MW01670763

THE LUG OF DAYS TO COME

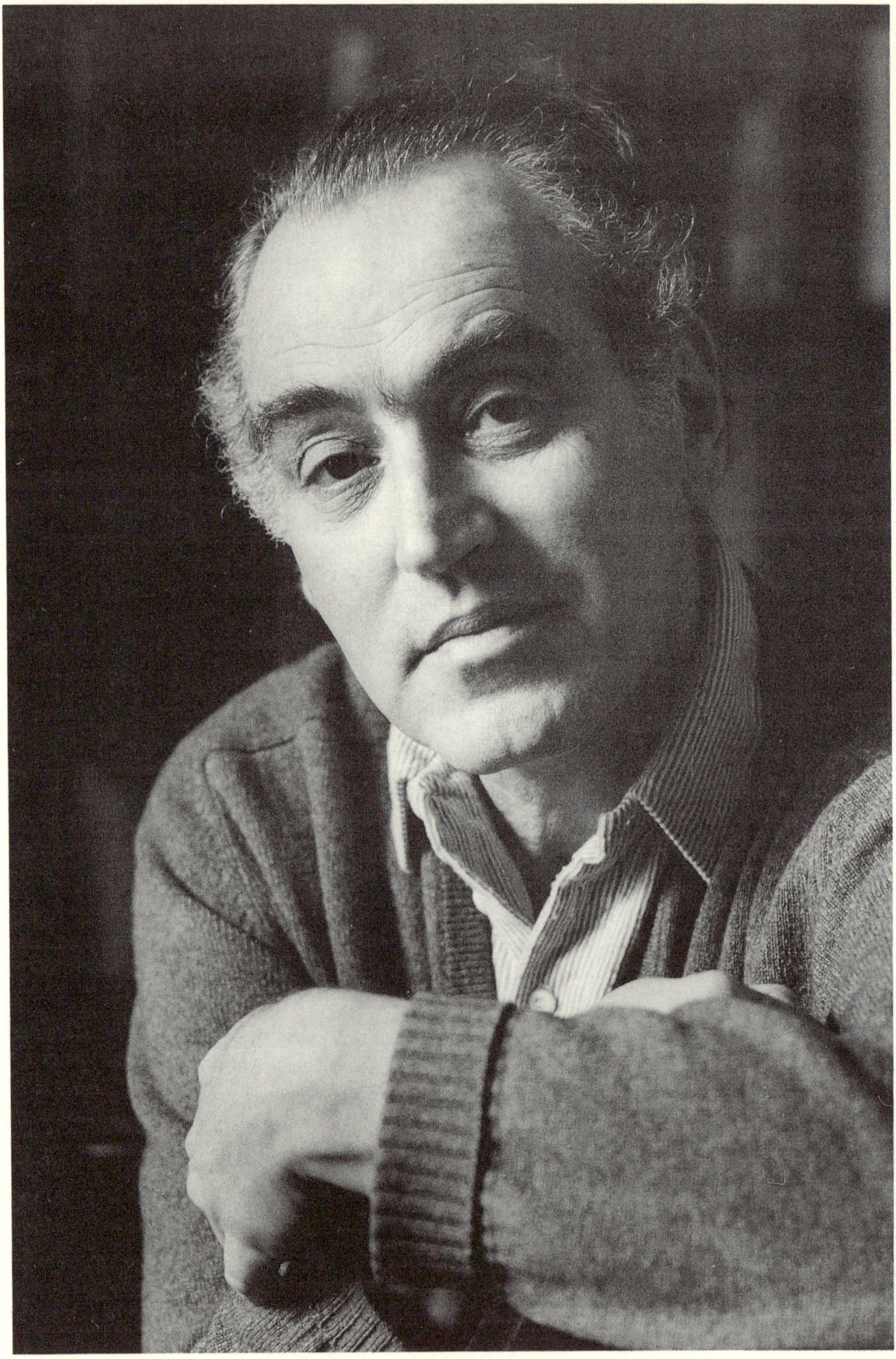

The Lug of Days to Come

New and Selected Poems and Translations

DANIEL HABERMAN

FOREWORD BY GUY DAVENPORT

ETCHINGS BY JAN STUSSY

JOHN DANIEL AND COMPANY | SANTA BARBARA, 1996

Copyright © 1996 by Barbara Nissman Haberman
All Rights Reserved
Printed in the United States of America

Published by John Daniel and Company
A Division of Daniel and Daniel, Publishers, Inc.
Post Office Box 21922
Santa Barbara, CA 93121

LIBRARY OF CONGRESS CATALOGING-IN-PUBLICATION DATA
Haberman, Daniel
The lug of days to come : new and selected poems and translations / Daniel Haberman ; with a foreword by Guy Davenport.
p. cm.
ISBN 1-880284-13-8
I. Title.
PS3558.A23L84 1996
811'.54—dc20 95-13869
CIP

In memory of

Edward Dahlberg

(1900–1977)

How would it be if he had lied?

NOTE

Of the new poems, "The Lug of Days to Come," "Morning on the Orient Express," "Night Sheds Dawn Its Dew," "The Sky in an Auburn Haze," and "Clumbering" were first published in the *Southern Review.*

The translation, "Erinna's Lament for Baucis," is published in the *Norton Book of Classical Literature,* edited by Bernard Knox, 1993.

The translations of Archilochus, Erinna, Praxilla, Antipater of Sidon, Zenobius, and Gaetulicus were done in collaboration with Marylin B. Arthur.

CONTENTS

FOREWORD

Daniel Haberman was a man of just and exact boundaries. His editions of Shakespeare that he designed and chose illustrators for, each play having its own volume, boxed and bound with taste and restraint, are masterpieces of the printer's art. These wide-margined, large square-paged, generously spaced books, boldly naked of prefaces and notes, were given away annually by the printing firm where Daniel worked as a typographer and designer. I know of no other printing of Shakespeare that pays him such honor, or emphasizes so beautifully the integrity and uniqueness of each of the plays.

The public, however, knows Daniel Haberman as the poet in residence at the Cathedral of St. John the Divine, where he instituted the American Poets' Corner and served as chairman of the board of electors who choose two poets every year in a ceremony of readings and encomiums which have increasingly become events attracting national attention. Daniel found a space for American poetry to be honored and celebrated, and as with his Shakespeare, by means of fine lettering and exact boundaries, using two storehouses of the spirit, the book-shelf and a cathedral.

As long as I knew him, through letters only, he was over the years always concerned with space and boundaries: his New York apartment, a farm in Ireland, and the house in West Virginia where his widow, the concert pianist and brilliant interpreter of Liszt and Prokofieff, still lives.

His final boundary, death, "the furtive wall," as he called it in a moving poem, he encountered in August 1991, in his fifty-eighth year. He knew through a long and brave illness that the furtive wall was very near, and gathered up his poems, making revisions and adjustments. My copy of the manuscript has notes to me throughout, the kind of shop talk about accuracy in translation or the justness of an adjective that we had exchanged in letters over many years. Our meeting ground was the soldier poet Archilochus, in whom we both found an inexhaustible interest.

A critic has said recently that there are now too many poets, that nobody can keep up with their work, that they write for each other, that they have enviable university posts where they lead the good life as imposters and lazy tricksters. Daniel, always concerned about boundaries, would have been sympathetic with this perennial complaint insofar as it's saying that the crowds of the untalented confuse our view of the talented, but he would have known that time, that fine critic, would sort things out. The Muse is a jealous mistress.

Ezra Pound ends his Chinese cantos with praise for an emperor who also wrote poems. "Perhaps you will look up his verses." *They* have survived, and for a reason. History sifts, finds, keeps. A culture with too many poets is cause, perhaps, for congratulation rather than complaint. That a culture has poetry as a means for focusing thought, shaping emotion, and fighting the good fight (as witness the use of poetry by all the factions in current political and ideological discourse) sounds like a good thing.

Daniel Haberman, who wrote with restraint, wrote in constant awe of poets he admired, especially those in the deep past and at the beginnings of European poetry. He saw poetry as a hard craft to be mastered. He was not one to sculpt in putty and call it stone. His *Poems* came out in 1977, and had a second edition in 1982. He published several small-press limited editions of Greek poetry, in collaboration with Marylin B. Arthur. *The Furtive Wall,* with etchings by Jan Stussy, came out in 1982. *The Lug of Days to Come—New and Selected Poems* is in effect his life's work, revised, pared down, subjected to his own severe demands on himself. A poet who worked under the eye of Edward Dahlberg is not easy on himself.

Phrases shaped with classical exactitude *(the banking geese heel)*, the unexpected but perfect adjective *(the lanky field)*, the image in motion *(preening glance—latticing down)*, a suave handling of rhythm and pace *(And I wander in the wait of night / And I wonder where the wrong began)*: Daniel Haberman's poems are first of all essences achieved by compression and precision.

In an age when we have been asking for most of the century, "Yes, but is it painting? Is it music? Is it sculpture?" it is intensely pleasing to find an artist who returns to or invents afresh a long tradition without the least use of pastiche. Pound ended his days writing in metre and rhyme, Stravinsky kept returning to the Baroque, Picasso's last decade was a meditation on the tradition from which he had so radically departed.

Haberman wrote charmed and charming poems in which he could modulate a range of sensibilities. His lyrics sing, his epigrams bite. He could establish the mood of a poem with a few deft opening words, and he could sustain and develop the mood to its rounding out. All that we can ask of any poet is that he be master of his craft (all else is grace and genius); of Haberman's mastery there is no doubt. Grace abounds, and in a phrase here, a perfect rhythm there, in a delightfully surprising pattern of words, there is the flash of genius.

His love poems are about being in love rather than falling in love; that is, about responsibility, caring, and cherishing. His mind was mature, skeptical, philosophical. He lived, as we all do, in a fearful world, and knew that being human meant being beset by anxiety and deviled by doubt. The fearful world was also beautiful and rich in meaning. Writing poems was but one of the skills with which Daniel Haberman shaped his world and his life, but it is the one which, when those he loved and knew come in their time to the furtive wall, will last.

GUY DAVENPORT

THE LUG OF DAYS TO COME

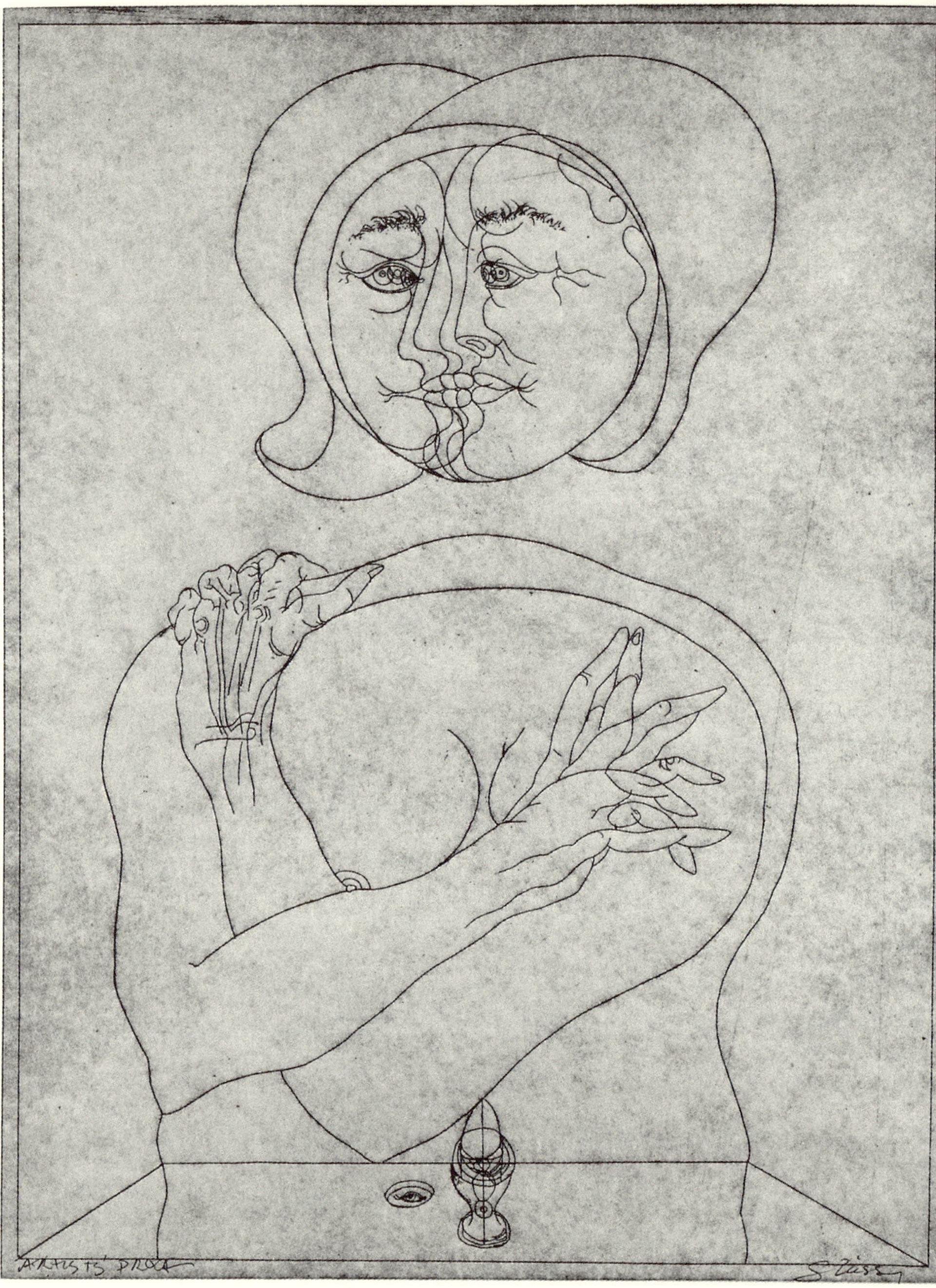

POEMS
(1977)

You are doubtless like myself; you have the same terrifying and tedious depths

GUSTAVE FLAUBERT

SONNET IN THE WAR METER

If I write a poem; is it not mine to keep?
Do I really have to share it? intruded on.
Unsharing; I'm an expert at living alone
And dueling with slow silence in the thorough day.
Euphony-loved and book-cared, though empty delight,
I'm not at all sure I'd want to be with me!
For I have many thoughts I no longer share,
Since he secreted them to a distant time.
He carried off my secrets to a garish maze
(No less unkind – not knowing he'd impaired).
Exposed as Isaac: I stood upon a stage
And, laughter besieged, I began to live unshared.
Do we all share such secrets when we failing-care?
Do I live alone, and unsharing, share?

A CHANCE CONVERSATION WITH ROBERT FROST

To the fields of Tuscany I'd go,
Where no language barriers appear.
A hilltop higher to a mountain ridge,
Where I walk in the same field of yellow
And I drink from the same waterfall,
While my old friend the cuckoo reassures:
Farmers are farmers – daffodils yellow;
Apple blossoms still blossom whitest white.
I have never seen a more gentle place,
Though I think I've been here many times.
By an old old stream the map calls Nestor,
(Do you believe in coincidence?)
Horace provides the sweetest of pillows
And, one yellow buttercup in my hair,
I drift away in Tuscany…

"Poet: still alone?…What're you doing here?
What's here in a field on a mountaintop;
By old streams of Tuscany?"

"I remember a more gentle time,
So languished by fleeted memory:
I had picked nameless ones; and sprigs of
Apple blossoms that blossomed whitest white.
Over there: beyond the stream called Nestor;
Past the daisies –
                    '…a swinger of birches!
Climbing limb by limb up a chestnut tree;
Proud as only a young boy is smug
When he's climbed the top of the tallest one…'
A fertile time in a fertile field;
When not yet smitten by puberty
Or Romulus' fraternal night,
He doesn't know he's climbed his highest height.
Oh, you were right!…I think you were right."

"I don't know where it's likely to go better."

THE REMAINDERMEN

Forgive the remaindermen, whose
Hireling hearts are beyond
The time of turning back;
Whose besieging hearts are appositioned
To the backward years;
And dream – O dream, now and then –
Of a time when Love believed:
And no one asked why
The commitment to soft her.

LOITERING HILL

The other day – near Loitering Hill –
Green by the grass – in pranced review –
I saw my past – and pondered why
It was to be my future too.

NOW TIME DRIFTS AND WORLDS WHINE

Now time drifts and worlds whine
By the weeds of inanition –
Which skive my soul paring down:
Rutting things shed themselves
Like a craning vine in keening soil.

A PILGRIMED SOUL

There is a time of unsweet regress.

Who then believes in coincidence
With sophistication beyond our years?
Temptation rises to hate that womb;
        And stay the time when I appeared
        To love the world in innocence.
That bloated carnage scowls me mute;
And what innocence dared not demand
Cast round my scanned and pilgrimed soul.

AT THE CHILDREN'S BEACH

I went sailing once,
Beyond the curling sea!
And when I came to my own shore –
It staggered me.

With studded fear I gazed about,
Not knowing what to do;
And strode the beach incessantly –
But seeking only me.

I rubbed my eyes with wonderment:
To see a man appear.
He was the kind to lose one's self –
Then I exhausted fear.

And daffodils – cupped with tears –
Now are waiting near.

AN UNRULY THING WHEN NO PLACE TO GO

An unruly thing when no place to go,
    The quiet of my house is heard within:
    Indicters crowd in the whispering air
    And embarrass a silence of late day.
I am but a madman, squatting naked
    In the nearing night, and I wonder that
    I'll not be allowed to invent my time,
    But shiver in fear of my self-same tongue.
Uncunning, my wretched mind admitted
    The garbaged poems which deceived the gulls
    Who screech and scatter in the cloud-dim sky.
Are these carrion thought of small despair?
    Yet I'd walk wilder in a gaping wood
    And wear the mantle of the laughing word.

THERE'S A ROTTING IN ME GROWS

There's a rotting in me grows;
A bulbing canker of the soul.

At my peril I'd unearth it;
There's a rotting in me grows.

Reality at every point is drawn up from the unknown.
LEONE VIVANTE

UNKIND REALITY

I numbed the world in fear of feeling.

Now I, too, am too much in the sun –
Now unkind reality
Observes the baleful fantasy:
Gasping, I grasp the bottom of the earth;
Bloated, my bleeding hands are cleaving
to the earth;
Glistening, the garish sun makes mutants
of my thought;
Burning, the accidental sun rages;
There are no rocks to shield me, while cleaving
to the earth.

UNPARENTED BY THE BLURTING WORLD

Unparented by the blurting world:
Things disorient the plunging sky,
And weary to bed I take my thoughts;
In tumbreled night I desperate lie.

THE PRISONER

I am the prisoner of my poem.
For music heard I am denied:

It is the agent of my rage
And – night-hounded – I am confined
To the smallest ward of all,
The pacing prison of my mind!

I FEAR THE FOREST OF MY FORTRESS HEART

I fear the forest of my Fortress heart;
Beyond the lurching days when Love may end:
Where cavernous Time bewilders me
And scolds the member that won't mend.

LIKE A FLOUTING SPIDER

Like a flouting spider
Percipient pain
Blends a beaded weave
With knowledge –
And snares
Emerging revelation

INTERACTION OF THE FLOWERS

Petunias raise their lovely heads –
        I'd rather like to know:
Interaction of the flowers –
        While weeding, it's observed.

But I and you – we vine ourselves –
        Lashings to the ground;
And often brood the weight of us –
        Annuals we're not.

MOOD MUSIC FOR MIDSPRING

Though unprepared for the demise of May,
  When sudden summer is quickly sensed;
Though flowers yield their wanton bloom,
  Soon traveling bees are itinerant.

YOUR INDICTMENT SAYS I CANNOT LOVE!

Your indictment says I cannot love!
    And will sleep alone, though many-bedded!
    Woman: I'd wait for a natural one,
    And hope my love's a love whom I'd love.
A bill-of-particulars you'd present,
    With many a grievance to cast me round;
    Then levy upon your angry suit
    And marshall demands that I should care:
Are you not degree-ridden? – journal-wise?
    Acquaintance-closeted and empty-dined?
    With conventional grace and judging sighs,
In a court of Love you'd have me fined…
    Unshackled – without counsel – I'd appear;
    My own brief presented: I'll wait till I care!

THE TEMPEST

Ilona touched me! – but on the arm.
Her fingers barely grazed my cloth,
And now I know what Prosper knew:
Ilona touched me! – but for a while.

DUELING

"For Godsake, Ilona...enough!

"Then I challenge you to a duel –
But I will choose the weapons:
Songbirds at twenty-seven feet."

"Poet," she shyly smiled at me –
"Then I shall choose another field:
Dinner at home; seven-thirty."

LOVE'S ECONOMICS

And now, dear love, elastic Time heavies the air:
Waiting disintermediates the coin of Love!
Would you, a speculator, be half-hour late?
Time's inflation risk the gold money daren't raise.

And now, fulcrum of my happiness, shall I be
Condemned to feel; but not to touch? Dear love: I wait!

GLADIATOR OF THE HEART

Ilona, you are unquiet.
    What gladiator of the heart
    May give it but to thieve it back.
Ah, love; our love's a proxy claim.
    The years unspent with softer lore
    Brusk the age-with-beauty I adore.

THE WEDDING

Though dybbuks dance on a frosted cake
And bouquets of laughter line the aisle,
I precede myself with naïveté,
Clad in arrogance of the unarmed;
As I'm strewn about the garnished aisle
Memories crowd the jewel box of my soul.

THE DARK WIND SHADOWS

The dark wind shadows and I'm cold.
Her backward years rain inward tears:
A Ghostly figure parapet-walks!

I can hear what she cannot say:
What attracts is what repulses.

Her changeling heart has avenues
Revealing where I cannot walk;
Now I fear the termagant years.

ONE ROSE

One Rose, glassed in water before me,
silently speak among raucous limbs:

Philosopher to coincidence
quietly, love.

LUNCHING WITH MY LATIN TEACHER

And now you tell me you've grown old;
And even doors are difficult.
And now I say, "Those eyes are clear;
Haven't changed in twenty-three years!"

Almost ninety: we're having lunch:
You ask, "Is this a tête-à-tête?"
Carrying on a feminine
"Shall I get fat from a butter?"

And now you tell me all your news;
Twenty-three years was long ago.
And now I tell you all my news:
"I'm writing, and...translating, and..."

And now you tell me, "It's so sad –
No one knew you were writing!"
And now I say, "I am not mad – "
I lie to you a gentle lie.

You I wouldn't hurt (no tears at lunch!).
You it was who'd respond with feeling,
And open eyes to Ovid-caring,
While poolroom-clowned I was hesitant.

Now you ask, "Would you read a poem?"
And say to me, "You were a delight!"
Now I remember slipping away:
Homer became adolescent play...

"The progressive ones knew what to say,
I just sat there in a dreamy day;
Your teeth were false – went clickity-clack –
Like lovely sounds of a streetcar track!"

"And did you not submit a verse?
I mean of course to English class?"
"Yes of course...teacher?...all!...But laughs
Denied: 'Fairy ships studded the harbor.'"

And now I say four of my poems;
You spritely listen – quietly sit.
And now you say in a dreamy day:
"Poeta nascitur non fit!"

(Yes, tears at lunch.) "Oh, Lucile – once –
I walked long long in the wood!
Where blossoms stood on appled trees;
Fairy ships raced the dappled seas..."

WHEN I WALK AMONG THE FLOWERS

I would like to anchor here –
Go ashore among the flowers.
But pirate courage are pistols;
Then conversation shallows;
Pauses are but silences
When I walk among the flowers.

DO WE HAVE SUCH SECRETS

Do we have such secrets to keep within;
Or would you agree we share them all?
In madcap times I have often hid
The stranger thought by a public wall.

I will not run with the most vulgar of all crowds, the literary.

JOHN KEATS

UPON ASKING AN IMPORTANT PERSON TO READ A POEM

"Not before lunch shall I read your verse!
The clock hasn't rung for Delusion's time;
I didn't come to your languorous home
To brightly listen to your putrid rhyme!"

CONVERSING WITH LIZZIE

"So you have a blue balloon?
Not even four, and it's fun to say…"

"I have a blue balloon!"

"Your smile is to me
As though I were three
And I had a blue balloon…"

But how does one get to be so small?
By not being four, I should guess.
For God and Goddess we pranced no less;
Not in vain remembered and still enthralled.

In the second barbarism, after the attempt at democracy, though they throng together, they will live like wild beasts in a deep solitude of spirit; and will, scarcely any two of them, be able to come to understanding... like base savages under soft words and embraces.

GIAMBATTISTA VICO

THE UNKIND FLOURISH

In a Babel world of loving
Our self-love – I cannot hear you!
Fatigued inertia fortifies
The new religion; and benumbed
By an impercipient age,
We are led by those we lead.
Not even old doubting Dante
Is relevant; as the craven
Pursue the license of the Self:
Only the unkind flourish
When mere thought leaves the floating words.

IN THE SECOND BARBARISM

Again the sun runs round our earth.

As gorged with import we demand
Scrubbings of our authority:
Emergings of the towered Self,
Stiflings of mediocrity;

We'd grasp the sureness of opinion,
Expunge the doubting of the soul,
Obviate what is obvious
We are unformed and little more.

GROSSE FUGE IN B FLAT MAJOR

beyond allocable Time,
Where madness screeches through a steepled street:
The Virgin bless the sweeter child,
And unchide the dissonant hours.

O give me time beyond all thought!
Where strident sounds of the muted years
Are lost in cathedral embarrassment –
And no mad quartet is allocate.

THE FLUTED BIRD

Inside me: a dog barks all night
Far on a winter road,
A fluted bird comes to visit
When friends are often want;
Then I'd walk back along the path
And trod the ways we came.

THE FUNGIBLE TIDE

Timbered memories flood the fungible tide,
As then, undammed, the poet rides the river;
And is not.

TRANSLATIONS

Or dig in Grecian Mines for purer Ore…
And choose an Author as you choose a Friend…
No Longer his Interpreter, but He…

WENTWORTH DILLON

Erinna lived in the southeastern Aegean and probably wrote during the fourth century B.C. *The ancients regarded the nineteen-year-old as second only to Sappho among women poets. Fragments of the poem were discovered in 1928.*

ERINNA'S LAMENT FOR BAUCIS

. . . Deep into the wave you raced,
Leaping from white horses,
Whirling the night on running feet.
But loudly I shouted, "Dearest,
You're mine!" Then you, the Tortoise,
Skipping, ran to the rutted garth
Of the great court. These things I
Lament and sorrow, sad Baucis.
These are for me, O Maiden,
Warm trails back through my heart:
Joy, once filled, smoulders in ash;
Young, in rooms without a care,
We held our miming dolls – girls
In the pretense of young brides
(And the toward-dawn-mother
Lotted wool to tending women,
Calling Baucis to salt the meat);
O, what trembling when we were small
And fear was brought by MORMO –
Huge of ear up on her head,
With four feet walking, always
Changing from face to other.

But mounted in the bed of
Your husband, dearest Baucis,
You forgot things heard from mother,
While still the littler child.
Fast Aphrodite set your
Forgetful heart. So I lament,
Neglecting though your obsequies:
Unprofaned, my feet may not leave
And my naked hair's not loosed abroad,
No lighted eye may disgrace your corpse
And in this house, O my Baucis,
Purpling shame grips me about.
Wretched Erinna! Nineteen,
I moan with a blush to grieve....
Old women voice the mortal bloom....
One cries out the lamenting flame....
Hymen!...O Hymenaeus!...
While the night whirls unvoiced
Darkness is on my eyes...

Antipater, who wrote during the second century B.C., *lived in the city of Sidon in Phœnicia.*

ANTIPATER OF SIDON ON ERINNA

Erinna's words are few – no excess in her song,
Her little epic chanced the lotting of the Muse;
For her remembrance – no music ceased away
Or black in the bind of night's shadowy wing.

Yet we, the countless fashioned throng of poets,
Lie rotting, Stranger – battalioned in forgetfulness:
The croaking jackdaws scattered in the springtime clouds
Are as nothing to the soft murmurs of the swan.

Archilochus, a wandering mercenary from the island of Paros in the south Aegean whose name means "first sergeant," wrote during the eighth or seventh century B.C. *This poem, discovered in 1964, is his longest extant fragment. It is known as "The Cologne Epode."*

ARCHILOCHUS SEDUCING

... "Contain yourself! I, too, endure!
Ah, calm yourself – although,
If hurried, and the spirit goads,
There is a waiting virgin here,
Gentle of the lovelier strain;
Soft with desire – she'd marry now...
Indeed, her sorrows are for you
Though faultless do I find her form."

Then I countered things she'd said:
"O daughter of Amphimedo
(Now remembered – noble and wise –
There in the bind of darkening earth),
The ample goddess brings delights
Apart from the divine affair;
Of these, young men may be sufficed...
Let's council with the willing gods
And, when all the shadows blacken,
At our leisure, take our pleasure;
Though, as you order, I'll abide!

"I've known to wait with my desire,
Beneath the arch – beside the gate...
Ah, don't begrudge my course, dear friend
I'm for the garden bearing grass.

"Now Neobulé's forgotten!
She is – alas! – just overripe,
Another man may have her – fallen
Long since from the tree of her bloom
And the charm that she'd had before;
Raving in lust of satiety
This harridan flaunts her vigor...
To the crows with her! The neighbor's
Laugh won't be on a wife of mine!

"Ah, it is you I wish – neither
Dishonest nor other-sided;
While she is quick with anger
And many are her friends – urged
Toward eagerness, I fear
Lest the get, as from a throwing bitch,
Drop blind – and on the wrong day!"

Saying so, I reached for the girl:
Among a burst of flowers
Gently she's prone – then placing
Her neck to my pillowed-arm,
We hid within my tender cloak...
Tremble-eyed, as a fawn with fear,
Her breasts were encouraged; so sweet
My hand caressed – then I revealed
My raw skin ever-new; entertained
With intruded vigor: and gaining
The whole beauty of her body
Let loose the white force of my strength
As lightly I touched her yellow hair.

Lentulus Gaetulicus, a Roman consul who wrote during the first century A.D., was executed by the Emperor Gaius.

GAETULICUS' EPITAPH ON ARCHILOCHUS

Here, by-the-sea, is the sign of his tomb:
Archilochus! who bloodied civil Helicon;
The first immersion of a bitter Muse
Into the venom of viper's wrath.

O wayfarer, pass softly by, indeed:
Lest rouse the settled wasps of his lone sleep;
Flowing with tears, the keening Lycambes
Has known the sting – three daughters hanged themselves.

Praxilla, who wrote during the fifth century B.C., *lived in the city of Sicyon, near Corinth. These five fragments comprise her extant work.*

PRAXILLA CONVERSING

HE: O preening glance – latticing down!
You've the face of a nymph,
Though woman below....

SHE: Gird for the rock, O companion,
And the scorpion under....

HE: Remember the words of Admetus:
Give way of evil man and men;
They bring, we learn, the small delight.
O companion! – of good men, love....

SHE: Of the lovelier things I leave behind
Are the gleams of the sun,
Then the face of the moon
And the sheen of the stars
Yet cucumbers ripen with apples and pears....

HE: Though in your breast, like Achilles,
Your soul is never persuaded...

Zenobius, who lived in the second century A.D., was a collector and compiler of ancient proverbs.

AFTER ZENOBIUS ON PRAXILLA

For those who say that "sillier" is her and her Adonis,
I'd say this Sicyonian was quite a lyric poet
(Ah, that is Polemon's accord); but she, herself, Praxilla,
Has raised – alas! – a question: why are the lovelier things
Exchanged for vegetables? O, may one but juxtapose,
To the cucumber at best, the celestial firmament?

Perhaps Praxilla's silly, just a foolish simpleton;
Or is she unselfconscious, as we all might wish to be?
(Indeed, the root of cucumber cognates with Sicyon,
And lest I mention phallic – and is that now obvious?)
Tho' all of our new critics would have probably compared
The cucumber that ripens with the apple and the pear.

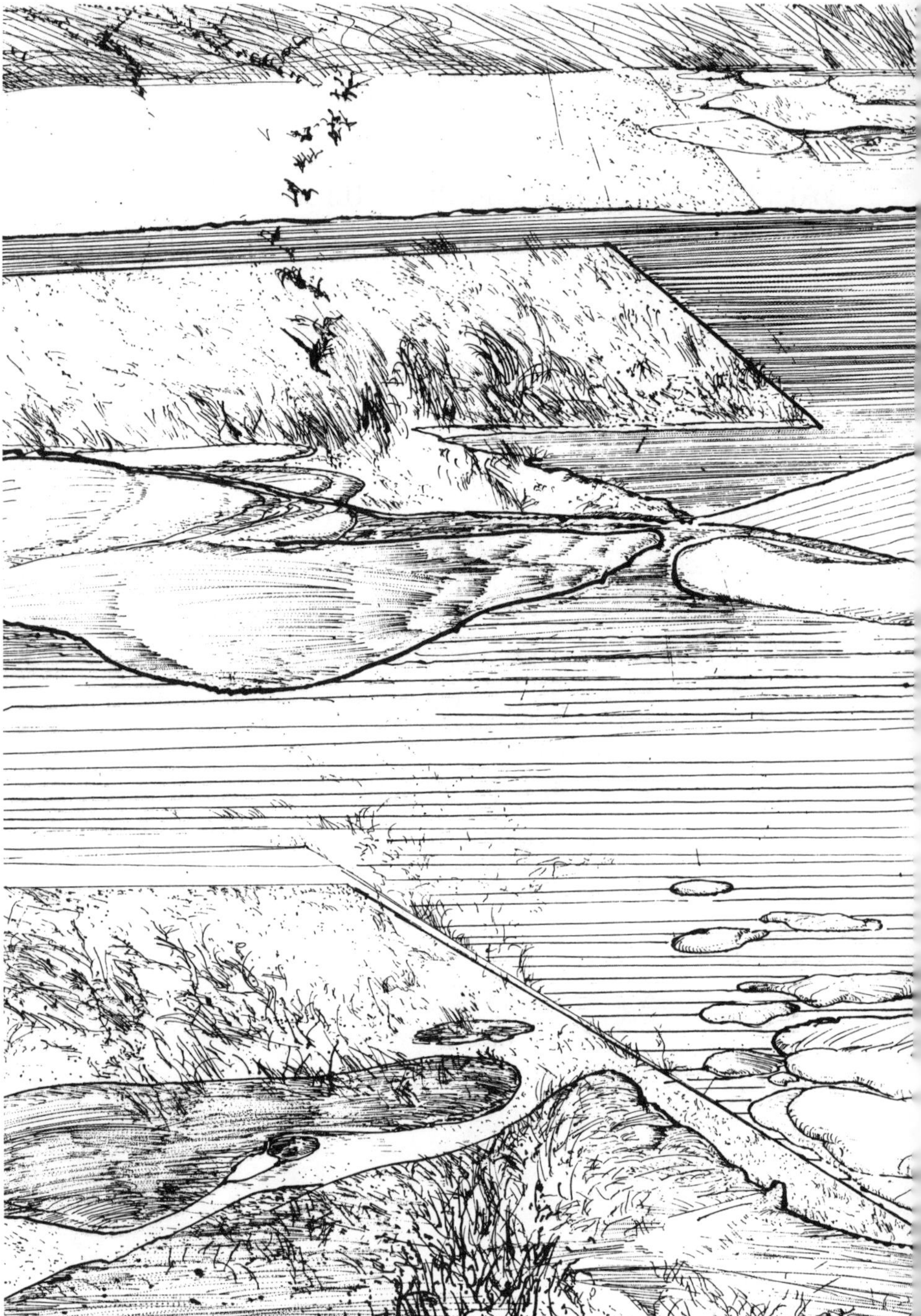

THE FURTIVE WALL
(1982)

And he who can weep can hope…for the blood around the heart is the thought of men

LEV SHESTOV & EMPEDOCLES

WHO CAN TIME THE CLOCKING HOURS

Who can time the clocking hours,
Who can time where day begins
When I have gathered-in the night;
When I have stalked from space to space
In all compartments of my heart.
Who can time the clocking hours,
Who can tell the tolling time
In all the rooms where I reside
And lie myself to sleep at night,
And lie myself to sleep at night
In all compartments of my heart.

THE FURTIVE WALL

There is a wall – a furtive wall
Bluely dark in among the hills:
Come rest your thought
Leave behind the wills,
Then go beyond
Bring your human ills.
I signal now a poising call
There beyond the furtive wall...

THE LANKY FIELD

Even now the russet winds blow
Over and over the lanky field;
Long, since the banking geese heel
And the tiny snows stray
Into and out a promenade of trees
While grass receives
The whitened shame,
Acquiesced into the violet same...

THE TREES IN GENTLE UMBRAGE SWAYED

The trees in gentle umbrage swayed,
Determined Time's no perch to loiter,
The dancing fears were unallayed,
The soul was weary of the slaughter;

Dreams were real – the real were dreams
And all beside I might have seen:
The heart won't mistress to the mind,
My heart's not mistress to my mind.

MIDNIGHT, AND A RAMBLING SKY

Lady, I cannot say I'm pleased with me
As I pare the gap of age and youth,
And I wander in the wait of night
And I wonder where the wrong began;

Lady, if we could now just have met
And Time were back to younger time…
But Love defaults to a rambling sky:
The stars lean down and quietly laugh.

A LETTER FROM THE VIRGIN ISLES

"When you have resolved what it is you want,
And can think of me in the tender time;
Then I'll come to you (in the tender time)
– Hold trembling hand to a trembling hand.

But now you live in another's house,
And walk with him (in another's house),
Yet cling to me with a trembling hand
And surprise a fierceness of my heart!

Give up this thought – leave me be – Love, I say,
Is a catholic thing: affairs are not
By Love construed as other than the world
Has known. Conduct your way! Compose yourself!
Woman, I say: don't come when Time is terse!"
He keeps the woman, while I hold the verse.

THE JOURNEYING GIRL

Go ramble in the lolling hills,
Yet stay with me this gruffing night;
You neighbored Love, O journeying girl,
In the fretted surface of the day.

NO CHILD OF MORNING

Let us say I'm sad for all the world.
Oh, let's just say I'm sad for me and you:
    You cannot change the things you do
    And I – no child of morning,
    Though yet of yesterday –
    I cannot stay!
Let us say I'm silent to the world.
Oh, let's just say I'm silently unfurled
    While whispering up a spiral
    And revealed – I cannot change
    The hum of you and me –
    It is easy
As the hero; hard to live a life…
Oh, let's just say I'm sad for all the world.

I SUPPOSE, OF COURSE, NOTHING'S NEW

I suppose, of course, nothing's new,
            though flowers are few
      in the heart of the world!
Except, of course, my love for her;

And though, of course, we are but two,
            she severed and strew
      in the heart of the world!
I would have been but one with her.

THE WAIT OF NIGHT

I, by-a-lake, face a scouring sky
And think of the time when Love lay by,
        My love lay by:
Delightedly eating – wine we were drinking,
When I and my love faced the scouring sky,
        The scouring sky…
Now, I, on my back, with a book to delight,
Think of hours to come in the wait of night;
Listlessly dreaming and noteworthy seeming,
I'll think of the time when Love lay by.

THE GNAW OF JANUARY

Bleak of the heart and hearth
I recollect myself
In the gnaw of January;
A little movement, so far
On the crippling snow…

WHEN LOSS IS IN THE NIGHT

When loss is in the night
And darkness glooms the day,
The hours drag me by:
The years would fly away;
The sea takes in the night
And deep receiving me
Again, again, I turn,
To the anchoring sea…

We take but three steps from feathers to iron.

JOHN KEATS

SEA CHANTEY

Chancing wind of a mild, mild sea,
The wail of the harkness is in the sail!
Gust to a time when I was free,
O chancing wind of a mild, mild sea;

The sail is luffing – no one to hail –
Listing to starb'rd – tho' helm's-a'-lee –
Caught here in irons – three steps to bail –
Yet the wail of the harkness is in the sail!

PRIMITIVE, IN MY PERPETUAL DAWN

Primitive, in my perpetual dawn,
I seek the sea edged by a sundry sky;
And flail watered notions that tyrannize
And monstrous bankrupt the lovelier word.

Give way of theories – they destroy the wise:
Accede back through the eloquent heart;
Give in to the clouds and the awesome day,
Curl in the sea at the edge of the sky

While tedious license stifles the past
(Ignoring music that inures the heart,
Ignoring language – seamster of thought);
Let the freer declaim! Mediocre
On the trolling sea drained of denizen
Primitive to my perpetual dawn.

COUNTY KERRY. AT THE MARGIN OF THE SEA

In a sea-dreamed cloister-house,
Lived by the walls of the night,
Lived with the fear of a fear
And the turf-side clashings;

In a sea-dreamed cloister-house,
Lived of a Time dismembered,
Lived with the old sea lashings
And no one to answer;

In a sea-dreamed cloister-house,
Lived; – though the night remembers
And unruffled flows the sky
Above the draggled beach...

RED HAND OF THE SUN HIGH ABOVE THE WOOD

Red Hand of the Sun high above the wood
Winters slow into the windfall night:
    I have seen a possum quail
    Talking to the nightingale,
Winters slow into the windfall night;
    I have seen a quiet thrush
    Leaping to the barren brush,
Winters slow into the windfall night;
    Would there be a fluted bird
    Howling Beauty's darker word,
Red Hand of the Sun high above the wood
Winters slow into the windfall night.

LET TIME, IN DISPARAGEMENT OF DAYS

Let Time, in disparagement of days,
Inure the soul that yearns to accede
Through regions of loss and little praise:
Where jackdaws winging caw the sky
And stult the cudding of the blest
(The easy ones are blessed, they say,
Not caught between two days, they say);
Where nighttime grackles wander wide
And strut with pleasure their behest;
Birching sentinels arch unaware
As enrageous claims define the field...
Bold shrubs align this blurting sphere!
O Time, who loafs to lose one's self,
How different is the discourse of today?

THREE BY NIGHT

I

The exaggerating moon
lit the tree of night
slow in the silence...

2

The febrile moon of night
descends the sky
beguiled by proud flesh…

3

The flouting moon
comes to the bed of truth
stunned the silence festers...

DAWN IN LATTER AUGUST

Morning streams path tides of day,
Closing flowers hide their sheen,
Stretching women search policy;
And sullen summer sleeps away…

IN THE EARLY OF AN EVENING

In the early of an evening,
    While the world was marking time,
She left without a reason,
    And yet with some alarm;

Her thoughts were all of going,
    She wouldn't seem to stay
In the early of an evening,
    While the world was marking time.

SONG OF THE UNWARY OAF

Little flower – of twisted root
How dare you play a singing lute?

Won't you know – the day's not right
To dance and sing in Michal's sight

Stubborn flower – why rise to grow
Struggling soil is teemed below

O little flower – bend your head
Give in! give in! enough to shed

The little flower – unwary oaf
(Stubborn, stiff-necked, foolish oaf!)

Laughed and played his singing lute:
"Twisted is a changeling word
How it's used is surely moot!"

And there he remained, for the rest of life a female slave.
CATULLUS

ATTIS

Mad – with the moon – on the Phrygian shore,
He danced as the night – the night which spread;
He wound in the night – and ecstasy fed,
And ecstasy grew – and the tendrils bled;
Though in her heart – his heart now dead,
The dance had ceased – only night was spread!

As Gregor Samsa awoke one morning from a troubled dream…

FRANZ KAFKA

GREGOR'S DREAM

Round my head – through a broken door
Weaving there – while I beg for more
Round and round – the listening night
Crawling me – a biting blight
Roaches inveigh – the waiting floor
No more – No more – Gregor…

I am suspected of something – it is in the air. There is something behind me.

VINCENT VAN GOGH *to his brother Theo, while begging him not to name the baby 'Vincent.' (They had a dead older brother named Vincent; and when Theo's baby was so named, the painter had himself committed.)*

VINCENT VAN GOGH

Madman Vincent! – why dare to dare?
An emetic battle couldn't be won
The other Vincent was always there
But not living Esau – to be outcharmed
And I would say I agree with you
Another Vincent was cause for alarm!

The study of the beautiful is a duel in which the artist cries out with fear before he is vanquished.

CHARLES BAUDELAIRE

ARTISTS DINING IN THE HAMPTONS

"Then you're giving a dinner? Not without me!
To improve my Art I'll leave a husband home,
And improve cachet with a gallery-drone;
Then delight in my canvas!" (that vanquished me)

He mauled them every one without mercy. It was easy enough to see he was an author!

ALAIN RENÉ LE SAGE

THE POETASTER

"Not without lessons! – you're writing a verse?
Come loiter on my euphonious perch
Twelve dollars the hour – unmetered fee
Often the *Village Voice* has published me!"

Daniel da Volterra was commissioned by the Vatican to paint cloths over the genitalia of Michelangelo's male figures on "The Last Judgment." He became known as *Braghettone.*

GIOVANNI ANGELO MEDICI

It was Pius the Fourth who ordered a cloth!
And had breeches adorn so he wouldn't fawn;
And no longer giggle at nudes by Michel (angelo!)

But reduce no Human Spirit to Disgrace of Price.

EMILY DICKINSON

AFTER ACCEPTING A PAINTER'S TERMS

Was no monetary deal! – a painting for a poem
You suggested we exchange! – a painting for a poem
How can a buyer come! – O Dahlberg was correct
(People don't change. They only stand more revealed)
Weak friend! – the bond was of other issue
When I did yield to a painting on the wall

Only those who know the ocean ponder death as they behold it, whereas those bound closely to the ground are more sensual.

EDWARD DAHLBERG

UPON LEARNING OF EDWARD DAHLBERG'S DEATH

Edward died – will no one grieve?
Chided friends – will you believe
He'd stroke the heart – don't turn away!
Chided friends – will you allow
Little lamb – who made you growl?

Daughters of Saul – will you perceive?
What woman would deny a heat
When Edward danced the saline street
O lady barber – will you receive?
(Squatting in the alley wet
Concupiscent thought is met)

Edward died – will no one grieve?
Chided friends – will you believe
He'd stroke the heart – don't be dismayed!
Chided friends – will you allow
Little lamb – who made you growl?

REFRAIN

When young – with opening desire
A closure they'd provide
Now I crouch rather low
And do my best to hide…

ALL ASLEEP

In a fantasy of my wilder heart,
As striven silence loots the night:
Edged to extremity while all asleep;
If the angry night would only weep;
Squall clouds bloat the quickened sky;
Ruminations rain on the ruined dawn;
Again I ask, and again ask why!

BIRD IN FLIGHT

Dear little bird!
Flown from the wildings of her hair
As a gift of Time that wends,
Glisk with delight a gentler song.
In the drift of Time the way begins
And Time unfolds and Time descends.

Dear little bird!
So zealous in refulgence:
Lilting streams and tumbling voids,
Drenching rocks – soon pleat the night.
In the drift of Time the way begins
And Time unfolds and Time descends.

Dear little bird?
Why disquieted, though tempted?
Why, arrogated to dismay?
With lamentation, look and pass!
In the drift of Time the way begins
And Time unfolds and Time descends.

Free solitary. Spirit alone.
Unbound probate, homeless on the earth,
Fly, O fly: on wings of weakness – fly!
Frail Jeremiah. Probate of Time.
        Dear little bird...
Time unfolds and Time descends,
In the drift of Time the way begins
And Time unfolds and Time descends.

THE WAY OF IT

With the futile snow of Spring
In the still light of my heart
        I sing to you:
Not for the struttings of the barnyard bird
Nor the clanging of his woe,
        Scattering the piebald snow;
Not for the wrappings of the grasping hen
Nor the stressing of her region
        To a one-leggèd reason,
                As the pyeing snow,
                Coloring to the green,
                Becomes obscene;
Where is the way of it?
Where is the way…
The snow fails and the birds to the north,
White in their flight with the skying Spring,
But yet, in the still light of my heart,
With the futile snow, to you I sing.

NEW POEMS

No man can walk abroad save on his own shadow

SIR WALTER RALEIGH

THE LUG OF DAYS TO COME

In the purple of an Autumn,
When the brook yet flowing free
Forgave the land an anger
Which seemed apart from me
As leaned from rock to rock,
That leapt a farther way,
I wandered brook to runside
And whirled the slipping day…
What rugged thing then drove,
Hurled up the other shore,
The lug of days to come
With the years of heretofore.

MORNING ON THE ORIENT EXPRESS

Have you seen Coppélia's eyes.
Soft to the night: expansive wiles;
Do not be misled (though passion's here),
They may glint in thought contrariwise
        – Say, have you seen Coppélia's eyes?

Have you gleaned her sudden brow.
A quickened study is allowed
By the tilting yellow of her hair
And a pursing wit this frame belies
        – Say, have you seen Coppélia's eyes?

And have you heard Coppélia laugh.
The comic lilt on other paths
Beguiles a star in open hand
Onto her smile of traveled sighs
        – Say, have you seen Coppélia's eyes?

NIGHT SHEDS DAWN ITS DEW

One drop upon a rusted leaf
Is torn from broken eyes,
It sits apart from memory –
A heart will need its lies

And glean the fictive, and its truth,
Though both a broken shard;
O where is inexperience –
Obscure, and wildly hard…

A flower cups one tear,
Night sheds dawn its dew;
Where does the flower weep –
To lend the day its hue.

DEAR FRIEND:

Two months it is since last we spoke!
How like a lover, though no lovers we
Became as friend – the rarer one –

The gentle nature of our sacristy
Kept the years with priest-like care;
How came this rage to the keeping-room!

If once I erred – though I say not –
After a decade of attendant thought,
Why not a decade, and a decade more?

WEST CORNWALL

Unequal to the seaward path,
Where coastal stone retain dominion
And the hoarse waves of an iron day
Whisper to the shrewd quiet wind
That Nature had no more to do:
For me, unseen the blossomed flower;
Unseen the hawthorne and the rose;
The little blossom, unnamed flower.

CLUMBERING

Clumbering in the umbered night
Isolate near the veiling dawn
Stumbling to the wanting sky
Here is solitude…

THE ACCURATE SKY

When the mist is on the morning,
An accurate sky at play,
Then a wishing then would matter
For the clabbered-rending day;

When the chasing mottled clouds
Are laced with fugitive blue,
Sure a wishing then would matter
To the child we forever slew.

THROUGH AN ORIEL WHERE

Now that Winter is here
        And the oriel latch
By a question bare on a crusted night,
With a lattice quite undone,

Lets the seep of a glare
        From the rotund match
By an answer clear on a changeling site
(O, an ancient rite!) become,

With a frequent leer –
        Ah, the question's catch –
But an oriel where, tho' I thought I might,
Yet in truth, not quite, be one.

THOUGH MILD IS THE WIND OF DAY

Though mild is the wind of day,
The year in its flowering burst,
A bird sang alone, denying;
I can't begin, but continue…

POST-MORTEM IN AN OLD GARTH

I am dead, and having died
I wonder that I lived till now;
Or so it seemed – while others slew,
Like sulking tulips as they tried
To wrest whatever they'd allow –
In this old garth that flowers new.

THE CERTAIN TREE

… And to the proferred sky
(Which intimates a sigh):
Unblame a wary dream
Of Sometime – Sometime. Why?

O branching, branching scheme,
While others climbing seem,
Leave me bare ground to lie
Where skeletal poplars lean…

Around, around the certain tree.
Below; entwined; up on; this tree.

SWEET SWEETNESS OF THE PHLOX

Sweet sweetness of the phlox:
Why dost astonish us?
Why boast pre-emptively?
Your time's uncertain, too.

SAILING TO THE ISLE OF IWOULDTOO

Deep now beyond the placid rock!
Deep now beyond the buoyed light!
Come now onto the curling sea;
Close-haul with me a brazen sheet,
Risk now the wind of IwouldToo!

Where now a thought for all's secure?
Where now a wish for Starbuck's hearth?
Tack now to winds of IwouldToo;

O fool! This wind is not abeam!
Reach now to chants from IwouldToo!
Here's now the rhythm unsecured!
Here's now the form in formlessness!
Grasp now the height of lowly mist…

O Lord! … alone
                        (ah, who's to doom,
When the judge to the bar? – but mild,
Mild wind, and a mild looking sky):

Lone now abaft of IwouldToo.

WOULD YOU LINGER TO SUPPOSE

Would you linger to suppose
Venus orbits as the Rose
Yields its fold to patterned Time;
Though we declaim on the sublime.

You'd know at once if I'd heard Prodicus' fifty-drachma lecture,
but as it was I only heard his one-drachma one!

PLATO

WRITTEN TO A PROFESSOR WHO HAD ULTIMATELY DETERMINED THAT HE WAS TOO BUSY TO ESSAY MY WORTH

Well, Khachig, this century's come and gone,
All the clinkered thought's been wasted way;
Yet wordsmiths wrought their ancient lines,
Which still, may clang within the halls of us,
While others sculpt their name: Ozymandias!

I was about to sing in heroic strain of arms and fierce combats...but Cupid began to laugh...we poets belong to the Muses. OVID

HOLIDAY IN LATIUM

(A PARODY ON OVID'S *AMORES*)

Of arms and the woman I seem to sing.
It's Spring and I'm on holiday!
My Muse – it seems a freer one –
She too demands a holiday;
We're off to Latium – she and I –
Over Tyrrhenian Sea!

When my craft was beached
I walked – alone –
Safe near Pious Aeneas;
But sad the stowaway Muse appeared:
"Father Aeneas sought sweet Lavinia!"
"You silly wench; poets need a holiday!"
"Poet," she replied,
As we walked the Forum at dusk,
"I know you well!
You're standing where Antony stood,
And soon you'd sing of him;
But I'll sing of woman, and loneliness..."
(And she smiled an obstinate smile.)

"When you're in *Milano* contemplating
Prosper's perfidious brother,
I'll sing of Florence, where Beatrice was:
You'll be lonely in *Firenze*!"
Why complain? – the wound is ajar –

What's wrong with me – I wonder –
Tearing before the Pietà?
(*Il Papa's* talk didn't move that much!)
Must be the rain – or the crowd –
"There's one!" I shouted to the Muse,
"In a stylish long skirt, trimmed in white!"
"Fool poet," she sighed,
"You're looking at a nun!
But it's Saturday night in Latium,
And goodbye for now – for three's a throng –
Put away your Pious Aeneas,
And delightfully wicked *Amores*;
Do you not know, to travel alone
Is lonely traveled?"

"Ah, too true, dear stowaway Muse.
It shall not be all Virgilius,
Or even the scandaled Ovidius
(To travel alone is lonely traveled),
But; tell me – please! –
May one be lonely for aloneness?"

THE SKY IN AN AUBURN HAZE

With cattle lowing to the hills,
The sky in an auburn haze,
A girl delights in her peasantry,
And the man would dance to a gaze;

Her room was ceiled – though night was quick –
And the moon flowed down the path,
The flowers shown of an ancient ache,
And the stars despaired for her laugh;

The boughs were veiled in spreading green,
The path was short – forever now –
The woman halted infinitely…
To the music of a lowing cow.

"But he loved, as the wind,
Where he listed" – she'd sigh –
"Dark is the late of night
Where the moon has soothed the sky."

THE TALE OF NAUGHT

Before the wind we lived at sea,
I cannot tell the tale of naught;
Though naught is not the tale I'd tell
When lived at sea before the wind!

Hanging and wiving goes by destiny.
WILLIAM SHAKESPEARE

A SIMPLE PRAYER

Then let me add a simple prayer,
And to its consequence I hear
A last outcry of Self expire
As in the very me an I
Is liar: woman – O lady! –
I love you…

THE NIGHT WOULD TREMBLE MAY

When there's nothing I've to do
And the night would tremble May,
The hills then lead on to
Where Time and children play...

Tell me please where I've been lost,
And where dark fields unfold;
One without, a path's been crossed,
Tell me please what I've been told.

Every epoch sighs for a better world, the more profound the despair caused by the chaotic present, the more intimate is the sigh.
JOHAN HUIZINGA

AT THE END OF A LATTER CENTURY

Though the shooting sprout of Spring begin
And a prescient sleep of bulbs is fled,
A silence settles upon the earth:

In a quiet of mere momentum
All sigh a scream of "never again,"
And silence settles upon the earth,
Blossom by blossom upon the earth;

Though Spring is new there's no idea
– No idea for occurring day!
And silence settles upon the earth,
Blossom by blossom upon the earth.

ALLEGHENY NIGHT. WEST VIRGINIA

Outward to the dawn-lit sky,
Where the bent birch shape
The bundled snow;
Where the willful cold
And the marsh-grass hiss
Of the spitting snow
Claim a wilder soul.

AFTERWORD

I keep writing poems. At some point I shall decide there are enough to make a book, and when that is I won't know until it happens. As for my themes, they seem to be ones of love, loss and the natural world, though I don't know which theme will engage me until I write it. This is why Robert Frost said that a poem "is never thought to begin with, it finds thought."

I believe, with Quintilian, that "the heart makes the eloquence," and that compression and form are part of the natural flow of rhythm, rhyme and the general music of poetry. I believe that poetry is the universal language which the heart holds, and not the language of the village barber nor something precious and unavailable.

Anything may trigger a poem: a word, a thought, a memory, etc. The personal views and values reflected in my poetry might best be described through my belief that the poet's occupation is the retelling of old truths, retold in a manner that might speak to the current or future generations.

I would describe all things other than making poems as a constant battle for solitude, that has always been necessary for the poet, composer of music, etc. This is a special problem in our century. I do not use a desk, a typewriter, or a word processor. I compose poems in my head or with a pencil/pen and paper.

DANIEL HABERMAN

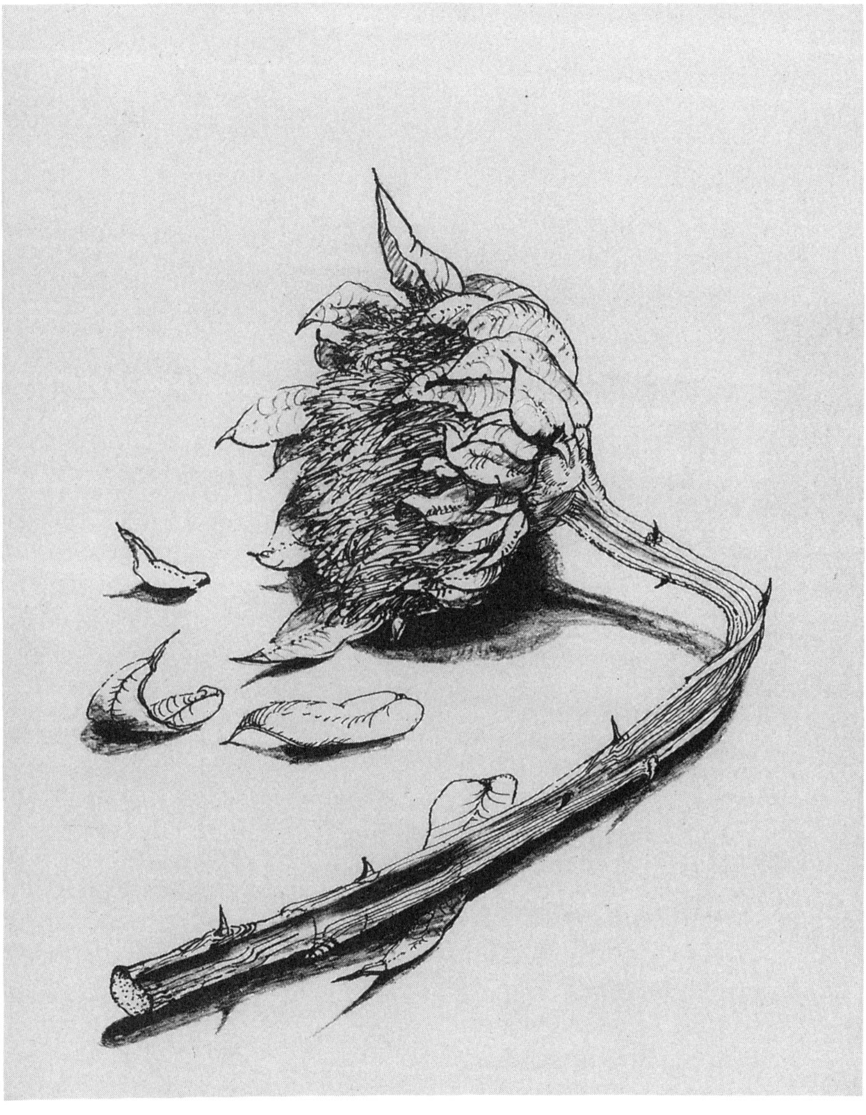